Wilma's mum took the children to an adventure playground. It was a new playground and it looked exciting.

They all wanted a go on the zip wire.
Chip went first. It was hard to get on it, so
Wilma's mum helped him.

The zip wire went fast.

"Yee ha! This is scary," called Chip.

"I love it."

Wilma was next, but she felt scared.
Then the wind blew and it began to rain.
"It's too windy and it's raining," said
Wilma. "I can't go."

"It's a bad storm," said Mum.
"Let's go home. We can come back
another day."

So they all ran back to the car.

Wilf and Wilma went back to Biff and
Chip's house. They went to Biff's
room to play.

"I hope we go back to the adventure playground," said Wilf. "I want a go on the zip wire."

Then the magic key began to glow.

The magic took the children back in
time. It took them to a cliff near the
sea. A bad storm was blowing.

Suddenly, there was a bang. A bright
light lit up the sky. Then a girl ran
down the path. Behind her was a
man on crutches.

"Will you help us?" asked the girl. "The storm has blown a ship on to the rocks. The light in the sky was a call for help."

"We can't help," said Wilma. "You
need to call the lifeboat."

"We can't," said the girl. "The lifeboat
has gone to help another ship."

"My name is Jane," said the girl.

"I'm Jane's father," said the man. "I should be out with the lifeboat, but I've hurt my back."

"The ship is stuck on the rocks," said
Jane. "People are in danger. If you
help us, we can rescue them."

They ran to the lifeboat station.
Jane loaded things on to a donkey.
She gave the children long poles
to carry.

They went back along the path. The
waves were crashing over the ship.
"This is a bad storm," said Wilf.

Jane told the children to lash two poles together.

"We must make sure they don't fall over," she said.

Jane's father had a special cannon. He shot a line out over the water. The line flew through the air and landed on the ship.

Jane tied a rope to the line. The
people on the ship pulled it across.
Then they tied the rope to the ship.

Jane's father put a pulley on the
rope. The pulley had a ring tied to it.

"I get it," said Wilf. "The people sit
in that funny-looking ring."

"Now we pull them in," said Jane.
"And I thought the zip wire was
scary," said Wilma.

It was hard pulling the people
across on the pulley. The rope dipped
in the middle and it swung in the wind.

The last to come was the captain.
"I've lost my ship, but you've
saved our lives," he said. "Thank you."

Jane looked at the children.

"Thank you for helping us," she said.

Then the key began to glow.

"I'm glad I wasn't on that ship," said Wilma. "The zip wire at the playground won't seem scary, now."

"Not even in a storm?" asked Wilf.